# Bears, Bears, Everywhere

Written by Rita Milios
Illustrated by Keiko Motoyama

Children's Press®
A Division of Scholastic Inc.
New York • Toronto • London • Auckland • Sydney
Mexico City • New Delhi • Hong Kong
Danbury, Connecticut

# For Yuri and Miho
## —K.M.

### Reading Consultants

Linda Cornwell
Literacy Specialist

Katharine A. Kane
Education Consultant
(Retired, San Diego County Office of Education
and San Diego State University)

Library of Congress Cataloging-in-Publication Data

Milios, Rita.
  Bears, bears, everywhere / written by Rita Milios ; illustrated by Keiko Motoyama.
    p. cm. — (Rookie reader)
  Summary: A young girl finds bears everywhere and counts them, one to ten.
    ISBN 0-516-22847-1 (lib. bdg.)          0-516-27830-4 (pbk.)
    1. Counting—Juvenile literature. 2. Bears—Juvenile literature.
  [1. Counting. 2. Bears.]  I. Motoyama, Keiko, ill. II. Title. III. Series.
    QA113 .M52 2003
    513.2'11—dc21                          2002008786

19 20 21 22 23 R 20 19 18 17                  62

One bear in the air.

# Two bears on the stairs.

**Look! I see three in a tree.**

# There are four more behind the door.

# Five bears in a chair.

**Bears, bears, everywhere.**

# Six bears wearing pajamas.

**Seven bears crying
for their mamas.**

# Eight bears hungry as can be.

# Nine bears running after me.

# Bears here.

# Bears there.

Bears, bears, everywhere.

Ten bears huffing and puffing.

I'm so glad they're full of stuffing.

# Word List (53 words)

| | | | |
|---|---|---|---|
| a | eight | mamas | stairs |
| after | everywhere | me | stuffing |
| air | five | more | ten |
| and | for | nine | the |
| are | four | of | their |
| as | full | on | there |
| be | glad | one | they're |
| bear | here | pajamas | three |
| bears | huffing | puffing | tree |
| behind | hungry | running | two |
| can | I | see | wearing |
| chair | I'm | seven | |
| crying | in | six | |
| door | look | so | |

## About the Author

Rita Milios is a freelance writer and editor of more than two dozen books and numerous magazine articles. She writes both fiction and nonfiction for children in kindergarten to eighth grade. She has her Masters in Social Work and is also an educational consultant and psychotherapist. Milios often speaks at conferences to students, teachers, and writers. She has two grown children and lives with her husband in Toledo, Ohio.

## About the Illustrator

Keiko Motoyama graduated from the Art Center College of Design in California. She has worked as a greeting card designer and has illustrated many books for children. She lives in Rancho Palos Verdes, California, with her husband and two daughters.